RECOGNISING TALENTS

Published By

Recognising Talents

Edited by Dharsheni

Copyright ©

Dharsheni - POETRY WORLD ORG 2020

ISBN (Paperback) - 9788194928867

First Edition : 2020

Book Design by POETRY WORLD

RECOGNISING TALENTS

Compiler and Editor

DHARSHENI S.T.S

COMPILER

Dharsheni S.T.S is a gold medalist in English literature. She has co-authored 25 plus anthologies and is a Star International record holder. Her burning desire for literature makes her venture more nobler deeds like compiling.

Mail id : dharshenisridhar@gmail.com

COMPILER'S NOTE

   "RECOGNISING TALENTS" is my first noble venture and contribution to the literary field. I take immense pleasure and joy in thanking "POETRY WORLD ORG." for their non-profitable and free publication services.

   I also take this as the right juncture to thank the division head Dr.Niveditha. My backbones; Srividhya.S and Divya.R, also my kith and kin for being there throughout this journey.

INDEX

ARTICLES

UNWRITTEN ROAD

Some days I'm meaner than my demons. Simply because I am. I don't need to justify it. I carry both the pleasure of Heaven & the pain of Hell. I am what I am because of what's of my past. I chose not to accept the toxins of life. It was as if everything unpleasant in the world was a phone call & I finally have the power to reject it. I take life as it comes & enjoy the little things. I found that the best kind of happiness is the one I find in myself. My body knows me, she knows now that happiness comes not always easily.

She knows you have to fight for what you love. She knows it's okay not be be okay & some days when everything feels broken, she knows she's got to wake up & do what she loves even if in that moment she doesn't want to. She knows she's beautiful. She knows that curves come with edges & edges can be beautiful too. She knows life is a ride & it can get pretty messed up. But she also knows, that the mess can be beautiful if she wants it to be. She knows no emotion is permanent & no situation is either. She knows her want & her wills. Above all else, she knows she's all she's got.

That's what life is about after all. The endless possibilities of finding yourself. Not living the illusion that a bad situation gets better, but by making it better yourself. Not searching for love, but giving love to yourself. Because the only way to mend a broken heart, is to love it again. We all are just weary, pretty souls, in a single bonfire, the flame of some greater than others. That flame simply defined by passion.

But sometimes all we need, is to just let it come as it does & let things go as they do. To be so in love with YOURSELF, that it overcomes every possible hurdle. To live such a beautiful life that death will hesitate to take you. To love your scars & accept them too. More importantly, it's about knowing that every single soul, is trying to do the same.

Anoushka. P. S

A VIRTUE IS IT'S OWN REWARD

"Virtue - a tool to behold one's character."

More the standard of virtues, highly revered you are in a crowd. Virtues and self-discipline are keystones to individuality. These keystones with stability in character is idealistic of being human. Anytime this keystone is subjective to change, the result of which any noble mind can prophecy. If we badge our virtues on the corners of our chest or imprint on someone's mind deep enough, any bland personality could understand us, only to his level of perception to an extent he had screened in our virtues.

Henceforth, doing something morally correct is much important than getting a tangible reward. As it usually goes like, "Virtue is its own reward".

Downwards on the journey of life, either we failed to appreciate our virtues on time or what bothered us much were the most depressing actions. Despite all the eyes around, if you did deeds which in the first place were respectable, prioritize your opinions rather than an appreciation.

Anyways, claim your shares of all the virtues of life. If all that you did, really added delight to your senses, it did add meaning to your life too.

Chill out & Chip in!

ANNLIN STEFFY A

HIS KING ↔ HER QUEEN

No matter whether in life or in chess, a queen always protects her king!. The woman is the neck and the neck has the role of giving the head of the house cautious direction.

A queen always makes sure that a checkmate doesn't happen and such checkmates in life include unforeseen circumstances, trouble, issues and all those dramas that happen that the king may not be aware of. The queen needs to step it up and attack and eliminate these worries from life before they attack and destroy her king.

That's why a successful man needs a strong-willed and smart woman who will know what to do when her man is about to get hurt. She acts as a frontliner so as to avoid issues. She acts as the one who pacifies the rage inside her man's heart, she does not allow her man to feel self-pity or any insecurity which may ruin his composure.

Thus it comes out to be beautiful and a perfect relationship that queen protects her king's emotional state while the king protects her by providing and loving her, being the head of their kingdom.

GAARINY. S. V

LIFE- JUST 4 ALPHABETS

Just 4 letters - LIFE.

What is life? - basic meaning for life is a period between the birth and the death but if we try to elaborate the word 'LIFE' then in simple sentence it means the extension of a individual human being. However I would really like to compare life with a coin. As coin has two sides; head and tail, it goes alike with life. It also has the two prime factors; ups and downs. I feel like these are very interesting conditions.

For instance if life wouldn't give us failure, awful days, some negative timings then would we be able to appreciate the success, joyful moments, positive vibes? Because we all know there is always something good in the bad. So does in our lives.

How about Life and gratitude? In this day and age some people live to show: I mean they live their life just to show it on the social platforms. But ask the real meaning of life from that toil who works har and feeds his family for 2 times only & still thanking his God.

Ask the significance of life from that lady who is sitting on the crowded street and having some meal which is already 2 days old and still thanking her Lord like "Thankyou my God, you didn't let me sleep hungry." As for saying it's just of 4 alphabets but in real it is even way more drastic. My dear friend, I understand some things are difficult to cope up but not impossible to do so. Whatever the situations would be, be grateful for the good and see how the bad turns into the good.

Is life really what we make it?

Ever been to special (handicapped) people? Just look at them & observe. You are gonna feel they are somehow more stable than anyone. They even have some disabilities still they act they can do everything because they turn their disabilities into the different good abilities. They don't create excuses like Universe has done mistake while writing their fortune.

And special people know the value of things they don't have so they value the things they have atleast. However, they know sometimes it's hard but not impossible. They plan, they execute and they succeed themselves. This mantra is not for them only this is for all.

Hardwork + full dedication - excuses that weigh you down = success.

You know it's totally fine if you don't have all the riches, if you don't belong from a rich family, make sure a rich family must belong from you because it is truly said that life is what you make it.

Hitika Prithiani

SAY NO TO RAPE CULTURE

Rape culture is a society where violence is seen as sexy and sexuality as violent. In a rape culture both men and women assume that sexual violence is a fact of life, inevitable as death or taxes.

Rape culture is rape being used as weapon. Rape culture is 1 in 6 women being sexually assaulted in their lifetime. Rape culture is telling girls and women to be careful about what you wear, how you wear it, how you carry yourself, where you work, when you walk there, with whom you walk, whom you trust, what you do, what you drink.

Rape culture is tasking victims with the burden of rape prevention. Rape culture is encouraging women to take self- defense as though that is the only solution required to prevent rape.

Rape culture is admonishing women to learn common sense or to be more more responsible or don't dress this way and failing to admonish men to not rape.

Rape culture is the narrative that sex workers cannot be raped. Rape culture is the assertion that wives cannot be raped. Rape culture is the contention that only nice girls can be raped.

Rape culture is the myriad in which rape is tacitly and overtly abetted and encouraged having saturated every corner of our culture so thoroughly that people can't easily wrap their heads around what the rape culture actually is.

That's hardly everything. It's merely the tip of an unfathomable iceberg.

Nileena. R

HAS THE UNIVERSE FORGOTTEN ME?

I could see her crying, holding her stomach, sitting lonely in a bench. I tried to console her. I sat close to her, put over my hands on her shoulders. I just told her that it would be okay soon and adjust for a while. She asked me, "You are going to be 16 now, have you ever felt this cramp at least once in your life ?" It was like splashing me with hot steaming soup on my face.

From there it started. Right after I wake up, I do my prayers to Him 'Will you make it happen today?" I have not experienced those tiresome hours that makes every girl flump back into the bed for the next four days. No necessity came for me to draw a circle around the numbers in the calendar. My eyes had never left tears for stomach cramps. I have not the foggiest idea that how pain would be. It was the God who lives above the sky who skipped my plate.

The reality made me feel that I was the only unlucky girl in the Universe. Nevertheless, I always believed that there is no death for my hopes. I feel it from inside my veins of heart just created hopes even after every hopes fell down in the sea of vain.

The years passed. But still my cloth has not stained with red ink. I haven't said this secret to any of my friends in college. One day, the time came for the vessels to make noise. When I entered the class, everyone looked at me with the sympathy but I could see the gossips flowing through their ears. It really stabbed me. Does their gossy gossips about me turn to goofy gibberish?

Is it their mouths that should become dumb or my ears that should become deaf? It is the roaring of invisible scar threatening me with the quake of my life. The walls in my room have become tired of my sobbing face and my pillow sees how much I had cried every night. I couldn't find any way to console my dad and neither he consoled me.

Why have I not seen the red waters still? Will my prayers fetch me the good news one day? When will the fenugreek seeds in my bag become empty? My parents are worried that if this continues who would marry me? My parents are not taking me to any rituals, locking me inside the room and go out.

The pitch of silence is raised whenever they leave me alone. The silence swallowed the song of my soul or it is the saturn rings that slowly moves around me? Is water pills dropping from my eyes the only medicine that pacifies me? Don't I get a chance to live a life of a normal girl? How long should I bear this cold ? When do the pores in the leaf of my life get filled with rain of red?

It was whom who rang the wrong bell in my life? Is this a test to check my patience? Is there any chance for rays of moon to fill the colour of peace in my heart and to swipe away the storm of emptiness for a new beginning? After so many queries, my tongue finally rolled to ask 'Has the Universe forgotten me?'

Varshini. N. T

POEMS

THE LAST TIME

Two different lives, yet so close,
What's in their fate, no one knows,
This is a story of two souls, pure as wine,
They decided to fight for themselves one last time.

They were like, 'Two Bodies, one soul',
Together they felt complete and whole,
But there was something like a blind hole,
A hole which made their life a living Hell,
Something on which they had no control.

They fought and fought, until the last breath,
They just wanted to be together, and cause no wreck,
It's just the society did overcast,
That they can't be together because of their cast.

Then came a moment when they couldn't handle,
"Let's be together forever", their love was eternal,
Then quietly in each other's arms they both rested,
All their love on each other they vested,
They decided to be together like stars and always
shine,
With this they took breath for the last time.
With this they took breath for the last time.

Aadirya Bajpai

RESPONSIVENESS

It's not just a word or action,
It's more than that.
Seeking world from our own eyes is what will make all
the difference.
The thoughts accepted earlier may go wrong for
today's youth.
Who upbrings change in society as chances to put
forward their own prespectives?
Who won't judge on?
Unless they try to understand other's point of view.
Being down to earth and curiously inventing new
definitions for older ones,
Is what will shape every dimension of world more
sparkling.
Responsiveness is what all required,
To build up clarity and naturality more than
hesitating.
If responsiveness come into being more wide,
Will enter a world where there's no corruption.
Where rape cases don't last and women have equal
respect irrespective of any differences.
Where there are purest souls and hearts,
Where hearts will not resist brutal,
Is what dreamed off.
It comes true if
Responsiveness come into being.

Aastha Prasad

RAINY NIGHTS

I am the rain
Giving him favourite companion in those dark, rainy
nights
Forgetting about all our fights
And touching each other through beautiful eyes
without any cries
All those bad thoughts just dies
And we also make fun of some crazy, fake guys.

It is Love,
It is happiness,
And a beautiful pair of dove,
And a pain killer to emptiness.
He is trying to impress,
Getting dressed,
Clearing up all the mind's mess,
And getting ready to undress.

The pattering of rain
And our romance in rainy nights
The way he holds my wrist and pulls closer
Reminds me of the love which is getting older
And he is becoming my life's holder
Getting a beautiful winter dinner in October and
being my lover.

Agam Sachdeva

DEMISE

Have you worried about losing a - stranger?
What makes you to sense terribly?
Caring for the loved ones is normal;
Why are you feeling for the third person's - end?

Heart is aching unknowingly;
Gaining the pain purposely;
Tears flowing gradually;
Expecting them to return.

Some may go insane for the loss,
They will be considered a burden - when alive,
But, they will grieve after their departure
Is this a natural tendency or human disorder?

Some souls are achieved in the universe;
Some souls are satisfied for all the deeds;
Some may leave with unfulfilled desires;
In every phase, they register their existence.

Everyone has to face death,
Between this destroy your ego;
Store more memories by loving one another,
Owe their presence in the present.

D.Anisha

IN MY THOUGHTS

I'm the kid,

With crazy a bit.

I'm the Princess,

Yup, a little princess.

I'm the Queen,

Battle hard the fields ruin.

I'm an Angel,

Boon love.

I'm the Devil,

Drowns the back stabbers.

ANTOINETTE ROQUE JESSICA

HE LIVES IN ME

He lives in me,
Each day and every hour,
When the sun shines bright and rain showers,
He lives in my heartbeat,
His name is hidden in it's repeat.
With my each breath,
He grows more inside me.
Everytime I wear his hoodie,
I feel the fragrance of his body.
He is in my tear,
The pain of losing him was hardest to bear.
He never wanted to see me cry,
Every night, I see him shining brightly in the dark
sky.
I know I will never be able to see him,
But I will always feel him,
I will always be with him.
He lives in my every part,
He will never make us apart.
Everyone says he is no more,
But he lives in me each and every hour more.

GURLEEN KAUR

AT THE ETERNAL BEGINNING

I see a way through
the sea of stars
Staring right at me.

My travelogue at the
Length of my hands waits
For its person to initiate it.

Backpack is ready with
Loads of dreams and
Funny wishes to be done.

And here comes chaos
Darkness of dilemma,
Times of adversity.

To override all, thus came
The moment to take a
Firm stance for my first move.

Because I felt this
Stern action gonna work right 'cause
Beginning will always be tough.

ISWERYA

SURREAL REALITY

You left me alone in the daring coldness.

I wanted to trace your soul and seize you,

But aterlife, will not allow me,

To take all the memories, I painted with you.

So, I decided to stay in the creepy darkness,

Where you vanished like camphor,

Still clinging and lingering in my heart.

Like fragrance, invisible but still around me.

Heartbeat never stopped,

Breath and soul never left this body,

Skin didn't turn cold and pale.

Eyes didn't shut, but I'm dead.

Alive, but dead.

Alive, but dead without feeling

Your warm heart against my chest,

Your wandering lips against mine,

Your big arms holding all of my existence.

I'm unaware and unconscious these days,

I fell in love with you again,

With the surreal world I created,

Where I live reminiscing,

All the sweetest memory of you and me.

I'm being oblivion...

Oblivion... but only with your memories.

JENCY KENNEDY

TO MY LONG LOST LOVE

Still my inner self dreaded

Losing you and my heart

yearns for you.

My soul is weeping

Inside, out of grief,

My unrequited love fills

my heart with sorrow,

I'm drowning in my own sea of tears,

My thoughts are eating me alive,

These sleepless nights hurt me a lot,

I had so much to ask you,

Yet, my heart is too scared

To know the answer,

Is it fair to separate in love?

Is our union a boon or curse?

Because nothing makes me happier

And sadder than

YOU.

KEERTHANA MALA.G.M.K

THE BEAUTY OF JAINTIA HILLS

Watch the abode of clouds glow

The beautiful greeny paddy field

Hear the peaceful winds blow

Here in Jaintia Hills.

Climb the tallest hills and trees

Embrace the peaceful aura

Come gaze and see

The beauty of Jaintia.

Fishes of various form and shapes

on the bank of an endless river

Rushes up and down the shades

of the fascinating clear water.

Blessed with beautiful waterfalls

Like Moopun, Krang Shuri and more

It's God's gift for us all.

Beauty lies in every corner.

From the tallest monolith

To the longest caves in India

Such treasure gifts

Can only be found in Jaintia.

People are welcome all around

Visit Jaintia once in a while

Take in the beauty along

Take it in with a smile.

LEADINGSTAR MANNER

NIGHT TIMES

Shining brightness starts at night,

Cheerful darkness change your sight

Day & dark is best in feast,

Like canaries in the height.

Exaspiration vexation hold you tight,

Flowers of freshness touch your heart

Life of darkness opens thee door,

Positive thoughts twinkling as Stars.

Gothic deals you dead of night,

Drowsy gloom make us polite

Twilight into solitude step,

Close your eye, as much as tight.

Darkness starts to fill my soul - but

I sealed you with me, just be cool.

You're shining my life, like flavours of ice,

Are you an angel in my life?

P. MERCY MONICA

LIVING FOR YOURSELF

Living for yourself, for those who pray for you
everyday.

The dreams that are the reason for your survival and
not only live but thrive.

Look at the mirror and if you are able to talk to
yourself without any remorse for that reason.

Smile for yourself not because others want you to
but for your soul, search deep, learn what's your true
calling and live for that calling.

Once you learn that even though it's not easy to let
go but when you do it and live for yourself, your
dreams and for few people who pray for you it's
worth it.

Live for your own worth and because your are worthy.

Roopali Purohit

DREAM

They told me not to write
How prejudice!
They told me not to write
Which twisted the fact that I overlooked
I can't help myself with thinking
So, I can phantom the probability
That no one can steal from me.
Dream! Dream! Dream a dream,
That no one can understand,
The dream that I dream of.
O, heart! Heart! Heart!
Ride and squeeze
The dream that I dream of
Let everyone see me to my eyes
The joy of my writing,
Never knowing that one day my dream will
spontaneously combust
I leaned on my writing and
My writing leaned on me,
Even if just for a while
Hoping time would heal me
Wishing the pain again.
O, heart! Heart! Heart!
Dream the dream that you dream of.

SAMRIN NISHA.S

THE WAY I ENTERED

Born on the lap of beauty,

And dragged to the bizzare society;

Wandering as a normal animal,

Once I became flea and hurtle myself,

There tired off; bored off my failure

Again I stood with avid - Now

Wanna be a lotus which blooms in muddy water.

Wanna be a cloud which never shower a salt.

Bizzare world towed again and again,

Don't wanna be there, wanna be between my kin

May be a fool I am, may be a selfish I am

I won't sabotage my impetuous life

First words on this bizzare animal (me).

SudHersan. K

YOU KNOW WHAT

A Goldilocks theatre on universe, terrace,
With no ushers.
The everlasting movie on the galaxy, the night sky,
With no sounds.
The world's pre-eminent director, the moon,
With no cameras.
The world's top performers, the stars,
With no makeup artists.
The world's matchless music effects, the sounds of
the insects,
With given no disturbance to the silence of the night.
A movie neither has a happy nor tragic ending.
However ends up befriending.
Neither critics nor reviewers dare to jugde.
But only the audience who does acknowledge.
And wants thee (night sky)
Let it be.
You know what?
Those audience who'd most befitting to the scenario
And who bounded to unbound the curse crucio
Are You and I..

SHALINI ROYEE

LOST SOMEWHERE

The day is old
I could not hold
Fight between brain and heart
Victory was made by thought.

Lost in another world
From where return was difficult
Memories from years back
made my mind blank.

Brain was tackled
Somewhere between, was I wrong?
the only thing that helped was a song
To return in to present, To never visit back.

Thinking it would be better
If I had said something else
But the truth is bitter
Now I don't have him back.

But only a memory
That stays.
The day is old
And I could not hold.

Tashvi Aggarwal

COMMUOVERE

Be not the schwellenangst chained in your prison of
life,

Be a eleutheromaniac with the fernweh fire of
freedom,

Baffled yet enchanted by the serendipity of the
glaciars,

Or a nemophilist lulled by the mellifluous komorebi of
leaves,

Wishing to unravel the mystic secret beauty of the
woods.

Be a fascinated vagrant awed by the stories of every
unfamiliar passerby

Or lured by the touch of retreating waves in the
tranquility of the moon,

Or a seeker wandering towards an undefined
destination -

Still numinous over the vales of lush green flora.

Because solivagant who believes in crossing
stereotypical thresholds.

A saudade may wet the eyelashes treasuring
wanderlust –

But let that not astray you from your expedition,

Be a wayfarer and unhesitatingly explore novelty.

For the ocean calls for the goal-thirsty thalassophile;

Nature donning the bruanous skies, the iridescent
rain imagery -

Let your heart throb with resfeber whilst drenched
in nostalgia,

Let onimism eclipse your selcouth of self discovery,

Extinguishing the hireath of yugen from your dismal
mind.

For, it's when the traveller leaves 'a home', can he
find 'the home',

Let the hodophile within take the ambiguous path.

Vaishnavi Chari

A GIFT FROM THE HEAVEN (MOM)

I am gifted with a divine vessel to get inexhaustible

love

Even though a thousand mattresses are new

Will they be equal to her saree cradle?

Her sweet lullaby made me asleep

Her hands held me with a gentle touch

Her fingers pointed out my mistakes when they'd to
be corrected

And wiped out my tears when I was down.

She has sown the seeds of good behavior in me,

Now, I have become a proof of her qualities,

It's my turn to rub away her tears and burden

With my gentle touch.

VENKATESAN. G

48

SHORT STORY

A CLASSROOM MISSING

It's student. I was filled with happiness when I was surrounded by my children. Yes, they are none other than my students. They ran here and there, threw papers on each other, fought with each other but these moments were just short lived. And then I realized it was all the effect of the lockdown.

There was silence everywhere. There was not even a single student hopping around the class or gossiping among them. There was pin drop silence and then I realized again, it was the effect of the lockdown.

There was a kid who spoke to me everyday he was so much happy. I was filled with pleasure when my children were around me. It was like my family. I was abandoned for years and then came these children who filled me with much happiness and made me feel like one among them. Those corner places of me were used as a place to hide during ice spice. I was a play room rather than a classroom to them.

Each and every day was something special to me. I would eagerly wait for my children to come to me and play around. In the past I was used as a store room who just dumped the garbages & waste materials onto me. Later came these children who cleaned me & decorated me as a classroom and kept it neat every day.

Those cracks on the walls were filled up by their art works. Being with them was the most happiest moments of my life. They would take care of me like a child & nurture me like a kid. Then there were the students who played around me, who ran here and there, dashed on me, hit me & would run around with a huge pretty smile on their faces.

My day would be incomplete without seeing those kids and nurturing their little minds with those alphabets and numbers. Years passed by and the kids were now grown ups. They realized the value of time & all became serious in their studies & yet I was helpful for them again but this time only helping them to have a pleasant place to sit and revise their portions and not for their naughtiness or playfulness.

Yes, I was selfish at that time, just for being a toy for them at that particular moment but it remained as an empty classroom who was useful only for their studies. And then one fine day, I realized these are never going to happen again as they were graduating their 12th class.

My heart was longing to meet them it wept like a child to see them again playing with me which just remained as a memory. Those farewell times where they sat upon me for the final picture posing with their dear and near ones made my heart fill with joy but at the same time it greived hard as it cannot meet them again.

I became an old empty room where people threw the garbages & used me as a store room. Days passed and I was growing old my heart kept weeping to meet them for one last time.

Years later they demolished me and built a new house in the place of a classroom. I begged them, yelled at them not to renovate me. I pardoned them to make me meet my children at once. But they remained silent & my questions were unanswered. Everyday is a blessing and this blessing was given to me because of my children. I was alive for sometime only because of these beautiful souls named children.

Yet again, I'll miss these children as the classroom has been left empty. And the happiness cherished with these children will always remain in my heart forever. Though I die, these memories will haunt me forever.

In love,

Your classroom.

Aishwarya Nair

LETTER TO A PART OF ME, WHO IS GONE

I know you're leaving. I'm painfully aware of it. I'm writing this letter to tell you, I miss you terribly. You are a painful familiarity that burns my insides. There are others who have come and gone in my life.

None have made me feel a wave of nostalgia and feels like emptiness. You are the sharp pain in my breaths from uninvited memories. You are the part of me that's missing. I wish I could see you one more time, come wapking through the door, but I know that is impossible. I will hear your voice no more.

In all our time together you've come to mean so much to me. You are my best friend. My life and all my dreams you give me hope. When I'm all out you are my pick-me-up. When I'm feeling down you make me feel good about myself. That will never be anyone else.

For the rest of time to love me like you do. And for me to love too. The way I love you, you mean the world to me . You are my soul. My spirit and my everything. So, I wanted to say thank you.

Thank you. Thank you for giving a shit. That you for caring. Thank you you for being patient with me. There's so much racing through my mind right now and it's over whelming. But more than anything I am just, I am really, really going to miss you.

I want you but I can't. I won't pretend that seeing you hurts. Just know, I will always be rooting for your happiness, just as you had for me, before it all. You are my life. Physically you are not with me but a part of you will live forever inside of me.

Amirtha Gnana Soundhari. V

INCOMPLETE STORY

This is a story of two lovers. They loved each other too deeply.

Everybody around them were little jealous and shocked to see their soulful love. One day the boy went on knees to propose the girl to marry him.

But here came the twist. Caste came in between and the story is still incomplete.

Neha Yadav

ERRONEOUS WHIM

We asked our great-grandmother, Meenamma one night to narrate us a ghost story while she was making hot Paniyaram at the terrace. She put up a wide smile and started to narrate.

There was a little boy named Aditya, a brat who used to steal snacks from the tuck shop. One day on his way to school, he saw a mango tree and stopped by to get the mangoes. While climbing the tree he realised he had run out of time. Then he decided to take the short path forgetting his mother's saying 'Not to use that short path at any cause.'

Aditya being lethargic started his journey, halfway through he became tired and saw a deserted house. He decided to sit there for a while. He was wandering around the house and saw an old lady lying down at the verandah, she looked very old and weak.

So, Aditya decided to give some water to her but she didn't respond. Few moments later, he got to know she was blind. He started his journey again as he was late for the school.

In the evening his mother enquired him about his day and asked for his water bottle. He didn't respond.

The next day Aditya took the same path and to his shock there wasn't any house but a graveyard. He was frightened and ran away from that place. While he was about to reach his school, he saw that lady outside the gate. While he was getting back to his house, the old lady was waiting for him with his water bottle. She handed over the bottle and gave him a chocolate, Aditya ate and fainted.

The old lady took Aditya to her destructed hut which was situated in Vepa Hills. His mother began to wonder where Aditya was and she started to search for him. Then she enquired to all the village people and one man saw Aditya taking the short path.

Shloka (Aditya's mom) started to cry and informed her family and village people about the disappearance of Aditya. Aditya's grandmother, Menaka told the family not to worry and took the situation into her hands.

She went to Vepa Hills to see the old lady. The family is not aware that Menaka knows Magic. Once she reached the old lady's hut, Menaka got to know that the woman was a Witch. She confronted the old lady but she didn't care.

All she said was, "I want to regain my youth and eyesight. So, I have to give a prey, a young fresh blood! haaahaaaaaaa".

Menaka warned her for one final time but the old lady didn't stop. So, Menaka revealed she was the "Goddess of Magic" and that she has the power to control and destroy all the good and bad magic. Menaka lost her temper and banished the old lady. She rescued her grandson from the Witch and brought him back to home.

Meenamma ends the story and we were enjoying our food.

(The truth is Meenamma, has narrated a true incident as she is Menaka: the Goddess of Magic and her grandson is the kid's father whose name is Krishna Aditya Kumar. Normally, people don't use their middle name and the kids are unaware about it. So, they know their great grandma as Meenamma and their father as Krishna Kumar)

K.Priyadharshini

YOU IN YOU

A small story about a small boy – YOU. YOU is a normal boy from Sanscot. He felt his entire life was full of sorrows but one day a small story changed him a lot. Here it is...

A lady was traveling on a crowded bus to meet her husband who was waiting for her in the 4th street and a 40 year old fat lady with white skin got into the bus at the next stop and sat near her. The lady felt too much annoying but she didn't open her mouth. This was noted by a co-passenger and he asked, "Why didn't you tell her anything."

She smiled and said, "I was looking outside the window and the air was ripe with the pleasant, dewy petrichor."

When YOU (small boy) heard this story, YOU realized that he is looking inside the bus (dark side of life) instead of feeling the pleasant outside.

If you think that you are in the same place as YOU then it's the time for you to change as YOU.

I hope you find something useful in YOU.

Sudhersan. K

HEER KI HEER

Heavy rain and flooded roads. The clock struck five. I was already late for my classes. I hurried out and waited for a rickshaw. After struggling for 20 mins in the flooded lanes, I managed to find a rickshaw who agreed to go, but asked double the charge. Without much hesitation I agreed, as I was one of those girls who wouldn't ever miss a class even if there was a zombie apocalypse.

As the rickshaw moved slowly through the flooded roads, my heartbeat increased. I was already half an hour late. As I reached my classes, I hurriedly ran up the stairs. It was already 5:45. I reached the door and out of breath I said, "Sir, may I come in?"

Oh! Sir wasn't even there. Only one girl was there, nerd types, always sitting in a corner. Her name is Trisha or Tishya, I guess, didn't have much conversation with her. So, I sat on my desk and gazed outside, the sky started clearing and it looked beautiful. Soon, I got lost into the scenery.

Just then, I heard a voice, it was her, "Didn't you get sir's message? Class is from 6.30." I

I reached out to my mobile. Oh! How could I miss that? I thanked her for the concern. She smiled at me. After a few minutes, students started coming. My best friend also came. Rahul. Always irritating me.

He pulled my ponytail and rushed to the back. It was 6.20 already, so thought of giving a quick revision. I put my hands in the desk to take my notes and to my surprise found a folded paper. I opened it and to my shock, it was a love letter.

I turned back to Rahul, must be him, always playing pranks on me. He smiled at me wickedly. But he came after me, right? Maybe he slipped it in my desk without me noticing it? A lot of questions were crossing my mind, when someone snatched the paper from my hand.

Oh gosh! It's sir. He shouted and asked whose it was? No answer. He screamed again. That nerd stood up.

What? I was shocked. She? Like really? She wrote me a love letter? Does she really love me?

Yes, I do. I said holding her hands and looking into her eyes. It has been two years that we have been together and it was beautiful and worth remembering. Same sex love stories are special, isn't it?

And yes, her name is Trishya.

Wrishila Pal

QUOTES

REMEMBER

All around me, I see where people running behind
undefined FUTURE.

***

When we change the way we look at things, the things
we look at will CHANGE.

***

The way to develop the best in a person is by
APPRECIATION.

***

If you have good memories TREASURE them, if not
CREATE them.

***

Little things always occupies biggest place in our
HEART.

Divya R

QUOTE

If anyone asks me to choose
A lucky number
I always choose your
BIRTH DATE

***

Let me heal you from your past
Let me hold your hand for the present
Let me guide you for your good future
Let me live with you for the rest of my life

***

Let me comb your hairs by vanishing all your
burdens...
Let me wipe your tears by solving all your problems...
Let me give you a hope that i will be with you by
holding your hand...

HARISH Reddy S

INNER PEACE

If you search inner peace by ignoring negatives then
you sure found inner peace from your soul.

SMILE

Many things there depress us,

Many tensions and situations trap us,

But if we smile, then all solutions must be solved.

PATIENCE

It's not a word only,

If we keep hard patience then sure we will get our
goal easily.

JAYASHREESAHOO

YOU CAN

Always remember one thing,

No matter How difficult it is or

How difficult it gets,

YOU CAN overcome and YOU WILL.

Kashfia Islam

***

WHO IS A WRITER?

Writer is a person who can share his/her

imaginations, thoughts and feelings to the whole

world through writing.

N Maheshwari

RANDOM THOUGHTS

The thing I adore about night is the stars that
shines in the dark sky, just like how you shine in my
dark heart.

****

Wherever I go, I find it uncomfortable because
it lacks the warmth of the person whom I love.

****

The night saves me from day dreaming about
my eternal love, but it actually didn't exist.

****

Not everyone's life is made up and end up
according to their wish or desire. Yet people have
to encounter problems and make a lesson from
it, which should be left behind as a legacy for
others.

Lakshmi A

MESSAGE FROM HEART

When you are weaker, you will cry, it makes you

stronger.

When you are stronger, you will not cry, it makes you

weaker

So cry to become stronger.

***

My days can be meaningless

But my hope won't be meaningless.

***

Feelings can only be sensed by heart not by brain.

***

Trying to forget someone is like remembering them

the most

***

Addiction is just an excuse...

Everything is a mindset...

If you want to do ... YOU CAN.

I J Monica celsi

BITTER LOVE

In the world of 'I love you' and 'I love you too', the care of how they carry out the promise of love, matters.

Meanwhile, the rope is to be tied at both the ends. If one end seems to take off, the other end downfall with suffering.

'The trustworthy can't always be Noteworthy!'

Nafesha Badusha

******

MY PLAYLIST

Hold on your faith, so that one day your faith will hold you from falling.

***

Here in my life of lock and key; whenever problem locks, friends will be my key.

***

Fear of music & lyrics will tell you the level of addiction.

Suja L

LIFE RULES

MAKE, MOVE and MARK - Make a decision according
to your likes, move with courage and faith. One day,
you will be MARKED.

***

When opportunity doesn't knock your door then build
a door which paves an opportunity.

***

Doing according to your inspiration will kill your
original personality, better inspire but don't make it
in practical. Because the world needs you and
completely your originality.

***

Make your mind, may it take up kind.

***

Snap never changes the situation. Once captured will
give you uncountable happiness.

Srividhya S

CLOSED EYES

Civilization is the root for every chaos.

***

Politicians and God are same, they have power to

solve problems, but they never do.

***

Truth is simple, simple things always get neglected.

***

Violence, hatred and every terrible things happening

here are easily justified in the name of God.

***

You don't have to listen to elders always, Remember,

stupid people also grow old.

R.Suresh krishna

தமிழ் படைப்புகள்

தங்க தாமரை அவள்

ஒற்றை வயிற்றில் பிறக்கவில்லை

ஓடி ஆடி படவில்லை

உனக்கென்று எதுவும் செய்ததில்லை

உன்னை மறக்க நினைத்ததில்லை

சோகம் மறக்க செய்தவளே

சிரிப்பை முழுக்க தந்தவளே

மனதின் நித்தம் ஆறுதல்லே

எந்தன் ஆருயிரே

தங்கம் என்பது விலை மதிப்பற்றது

தங்கை என்பது வினையால் பெற்றது

ARUN SARAVANAN

அவள் என் காதலி

புல்மேல் பனித்துளி போல் மழைச்சாரல் துளிகள்
வண்ண மலர்களாய் அவள்

கருங்கூந்தல் தீண்ட ஏங்கித் தவிக்கின்றன

எத்தனை பகல் இரவு சந்திரனும் சூரியனும் அழகு
கொஞ்சும் அவள் முகம்

காண காத்து கிடக்கின்றன

நதிகள் அனைத்தும் ஒன்றிணைந்து பொற்ச் சிலை
அவள் பாதம் தழுவ

சலசலக்கின்றன

செம்மொழிகள் கூட வாய்மொழி கேட்க அவள்
வாசல் தேடி அலைகின்றன

நீ சென்ற பாத சுவடுகளை ஏனோ என் காதல்
நினைவுகள் பின்தொடரகின்றன

கடல் ஓர உன் கை கோர்த்து அந்த நெடுந்தூர
பயணத்திர்காக

BALAMURUGAN SINGARAM

அவளின் நியாபகம்

என் புத்தகத்தில் பேனாவின் முனையை வைத்து
பதிக்கும் சொற்கள்

அவள்.......!

நான் வரையும் ஓவியம் அவள்.....!

எங்கோ இருந்து என்னை காந்தப் பார்வை

கொண்டு ஈர்ப்பவள் அவள்......!

அவளிடம் பேசிய மணித்துளிகள் அதிகம் ஆனால்
நினைப்பினால்

என்னைக் கவரும் நிலவு போல் அவள்.....!

பார்வை மூலம் கூர்மையான வாள் கொண்டு

கீறுகிறாள் அவள்......!

N.R Karthikeyan

காதல் மழை

கரு மேகமாய் உன் கூந்தல்;

என்னை ஈர்க்கும் மின்னலாய் உன்தன் பார்வை;

சில்லென்ற தென்றலாய் என் மனதை

குளிர வைக்கும் உன் புன்னகை;

திடுக்கிடும் இடியாய் என்னை

மிரள வைக்கும் உன் கோபம்;

என்னை தொட்டு செல்லும் சாரலாய்

என் மனதை தொடும் உன் நினைவுகள்

விட்டு விட்டு பேயும் மழை போல்

என்னை கண்டும் காணாமல் போகும் நீ;

இடைவிடாத அடை மழை போல்

உன்னை விட்டு கொடுக்காத நான்

வெள்ளமாய் என் காதல்,

அதில் தத்தளிக்கும் என் இதயம்;

உச்சகட்ட வெயிலில் வாடும் நான்,

சட்டென பெய்திடும் சில்லென்ற

மழைப்போல் உன்தன் காதல்;

வறண்ட பூமிக்கு உயிர் கொடுக்கும்

மழை போல வாடிய என் மனதிற்கு

உயிர் தந்த நீ;

காதல் மழையில் நான்..!

MoHammed Rizwan

உனக்குள் நான்

என்னவளே...

மீண்டும் எழுதத் தொடங்கிவிட்டேன் உன்னைப்
பற்றி...

கவிதையே எழுதத் தெரியாத எனக்குக்
கவிதையாய்த் தெரிந்தன

உன் கண்கள்...

சிற்பியோ

உளியால் கல்லைச் செதுக்குவான் நானோ கவிஞன்...

அதனால் உன்னைச் சொற்களால் செத்துக்குகிறேன்
இதோ....

ஆதவனும் மதியும் நேருக்கு நேர் சந்திக்கும் நாளே
அமாவாசை...

மதி போல இருக்கும் உன் முகத்தை, சூரியன்
போலச் சுட்டெரிக்கும் என்

விழிகள் எப்போது

நோக்குவது...?

இனி அமாவாசையைக் காண்பது அரிது தான்.

என்னவளே

நானோ விழுந்துவிட்டேன் உன் பார்வையில்...

காற்றிலே நடந்து வரும் என் தங்கத் தாரகையே!
கவிதையின் இருப்பிடமே!

என்னவென்று சொல்வது உன் சிரிப்பின் அழகை...!

ஆற்று வெள்ளம் தடையைக் கடந்து செல்வது
போல உன்னைப் பற்றி

எழுதிக்கொண்டே இருக்கிறேன்...

இனி எழுதப்போவதில்லை உன்னைப் பற்றி.
ஏனென்றால் நீ என்னுள்

நுழைந்து விட்டாய். என்னையே

என்னால்

வருணிக்க

முடியாதல்லவா...

P. Nantha kumar

முகிழ்நகை

இலையின் நுனியில் பனித்துளி அணுகுவதைபோல்-
என் இதழின்

ஒரங்களில் எட்டிப்பார்க்கிறாய்-உன்னால்

என் கன்னங்கள் அழகாகின்றன

என் கண்களோ ஓய்வெடுகின்றன -என்
எண்ணங்களோ

தெளிவடைகின்றன

உன்னை நேசிக்காத ஒருவர்தான்

உண்டோ-நீ பார்க்காத மனிதன்தான்

உண்டோ- நீ சூழ்நிலையை மாற்றும்

வல்லமை கொண்ட மந்திரவாதி

நீயின்றி பண்டிகை தான் உண்டோ

நீயின்றி அழகுதான் உண்டோ

நீ எனக்கு கிடைத்த அதிசய

பொக்கிஷம் - என் புன்னகையே!

P.N.Preieum Naermathua

இன்றைய வாழ்வு

தண்டவாளமும் மனிதனும்

தண்டவாளத்தைப் பார்த்து மனிதன் சொன்னானாம்... எல்லோரிடமும் மிதி வாங்கிக் கொண்டிருக்கிறாயே உன்னால் என்ன பலன் என்று..

அதற்கு தண்டவாளம் சிரித்துக் கொண்டே சொன்னதாம் உன் வண்டவாளம் சரியாக இருந்திருந்தால் என்னிடம் வந்து வெட்டியாக உரையாடிக் கொண்டிருக்க மாட்டாய்..

ரயிலோ, நான் இருந்தால் தான் ஓடும் என்னைப் பற்றி கவலைப்படாமல் உன் வண்டவாளத்தை சரியாக அமைத்துக்கொள் என்றதாம்...

- விசித்திரப் பெண்

B.Subhasree

தற்கொலை பேசுகிறது

காசோலையுடன் கோழை பட்டமும்,

செய்தித்தாளில் ஏதோ ஒரு மூலையிலும்,

பசியால் வாடும் போலி ஊடகங்களுக்கு

விருந்தாம்,

கண்ணீரால் கடலை உருவாக்கவும்,

மலை போன்ற இதயத்தை துாள்களாக நொறுக்கவும்,

சிறு கயிற்றினை கண்டு என் மனம் துடிதுடித்துப்
போகவும்,

தலைகுனியா தலையைக் குனியவைத்தும்,

ஆமையைவிட மெல்லமாக நடக்கவைத்தும்,

ஊர் எங்கும் உன் பேச்சு !

அதைக் கேட்டுக்கேட்டு வாங்கியதோ பெருமூச்சு.

உன்னை மணவறையில் காணவேண்டிய கண்களோ,

இன்று உன்னைப் பிணவறையில் காணவும் .

உனக்கு மணமாலை சூட நினைத்த கைகள்,

இன்று உன் புகைப்படத்திற்குப் பூமாலை இட்டும் .

இத்துணையும் நீ கண்ட வெற்றி அல்ல,

இதுதான் உன்வாழ்வின் மிகப்பெரிய தோல்வி.

படிப்பில் தோல்வியாம்,

காதலில் தோல்வியாம்,

கடன் தொல்லையாம்,

வரத்தச்சனைக் கொடுமையாம்,

உச்சக்கட்ட அவமானமாம்,

குணப்படுத்த இயலாத நோய்யாம்,

இவை எல்லாம் காரணங்களாக

விதியின் மீது பழி போட்டு !

உன்னை நீ மாய்த்துக்கொள்ளுவதை விட

அந்த விதியை உன் கால்களால் மிதித்து வாழ்ந்து
இருந்தால் ,

நான் பிறந்து இருக்க வாய்ப்பு இல்லை.

இப்படிக்கு

தற்கொலை

M.Tajdeen

தேநீர்

நடு நிசியில் தனிமையில் விழித்திருந்து எதையெல்லாம் நினைத்துக் கொண்டிருந்தேன் ... எந்த புத்தகத்தை புரட்டி பார்த்தேன்.. எதை நினைத்து சிரித்தேன்.... யாரை நினைத்து அழுதேன்.... எந்த பாடலை முனுமுனுத்தேன் என்பதற்க்கெல்லாம் என்னோடு இருந்த ஒரு குவளை தேநீர் மட்டும் தான் சாட்சி...

அதையும் நான் குடித்துவிட்டேன்....

மழையை பார்த்து கொண்டே தேநீர் குடித்துக் கொண்டிருக்கிறேன்...

தேநீர் என்னுள் கலப்பது போல் நானும் மழையில் நனைந்து கரைந்து காணாமல் போக மாட்டேனா..

தேநீர் குவளை என் உதட்டுக்கு சூடான முத்தம் கொடுத்து கொண்டிருந்தது... உலகத்தில் நானும் அந்த திரவிய தேவதையும் மட்டும் வாழலாம் என்று நினைத்த போது குவளை காலியாகிவிட்டது...

இப்படியாக அந்த காதல் கதை சோகமாக முடிந்து போனது.

Vignesh.V

www.ingramcontent.com/pod-product-compliance
Lightning Source LLC
LaVergne TN
LVHW090120180726
843489LV00002B/917